Arctic Dreams

CAROLE GERBER

ILLUSTRATED BY MARTY HUSTED

WHISPERING COYOTE PRESS

The Arctic is the area around the top of the world that includes the North Pole. It is covered by icy seas, forests, and tundra—a vast, treeless plain that covers 5 million square miles.

Published by Whispering Coyote Press
300 Crescent Court, Suite 860, Dallas, TX 75201

Text was set in 18-point Goudy Old Style.
Book production and design by *The Kids at Our House*
10 9 8 7 6 5 4 3 2 1
Printed in China

Library of Congress Cataloging–in–Publication Data

Gerber, Carole.
Arctic dreams / written by Carole Gerber : illustrated by Marty Husted.
p.   cm.
Summary: An Eskimo mother talks to her sleepy child as they go on a journey through the peaceful world of the Arctic and its animals.
ISBN 1-58089-021-0
[1. Arctic regions—Fiction.   2. Eskimos—Fiction.   3. Mother and child—Fiction.]   I.
Husted, Marty, 1957-   ill.   II. Title.
PZ7.G29356Ar   1999
[Fic]—dc21   98-45878
                                                   CIP
                                                   AC

To Paige and Jessica
—C.G.

To Forrest, whose curiosity is endless
—M.H.

Close your eyes, my little one.
Close your eyes.

See the brown moose standing in the meadow.
See the musk ox grazing on the tundra

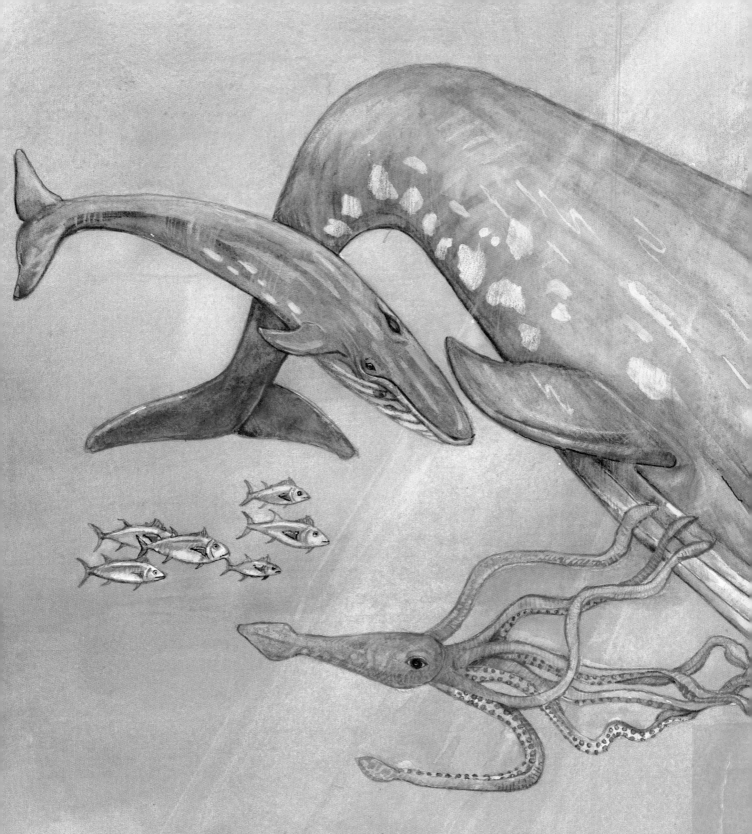

and the blue whale swimming in the sea.

Snuggle deep, my little one.
Snuggle deep.
Hear the roaring of the walrus.

Hear the honking of the wild geese
and the high-pitched calling of the terns.

Dream in peace, my little one.
Dream in peace.
Dream of boulders cloaked in colors.

Dream of great fields filled with flowers,
petals reaching toward the sun.

Slumber sweet, my little one.
Slumber sweet.
Taste the first snowfall of autumn.

Breathe the moist pine air of forests

and the icy air that blankets Arctic seas.

Go to sleep, my little one.
Go to sleep.
Dream of northern lights on Arctic nights,
wide bands of color streaming bright
against the vast black velvet sky.

Close your eyes, my little one.
Close your eyes.
Let sleep come to you as swiftly as a caribou.

Let sleep surround you as silently as a snowdrift . . .
and cover you as softly as the fur of *nanook*,
the large white bear.

Aja, aja. Haja, haja.
Sleep my little one. Sleep.

The words "*Aja, aja. Haja, haja*" are the common refrain of *okalugtuat*, the ancient songs of some Eskimos who live in the Arctic. There are many different Eskimo cultures in the region. Each has its own language, name for its people, and way of life.